WITHDRAWN

GAME FACE
STEAM & Ice

by Brigitte Cooper
illustrated by Tim Heitz

Calico

An Imprint of Magic Wagon
abdopublishing.com

For Steve: You fill my life with love and laughter. Our story is my favorite. —BC

abdopublishing.com

Published by Magic Wagon, a division of ABDO, PO Box 398166, Minneapolis, Minnesota 55439. Copyright © 2018 by Abdo Consulting Group, Inc. International copyrights reserved in all countries. No part of this book may be reproduced in any form without written permission from the publisher. Calico™ is a trademark and logo of Magic Wagon.

Printed in the United States of America, North Mankato, Minnesota.
102017
012018

THIS BOOK CONTAINS RECYCLED MATERIALS

Written by Brigitte Cooper
Illustrated by Tim Heitz
Edited by Megan M. Gunderson
Art Directed by Laura Mitchell

Once again, very special thanks to our content consultant, Scott Lauinger!

Publisher's Cataloging-in-Publication Data

Names: Cooper, Brigitte, author. | Heitz, Tim, illustrator.
Title: STEAM & ice / by Brigitte Cooper; illustrated by Tim Heitz.
Other titles: STEAM and ice
Description: Minneapolis, Minnesota : Magic Wagon, 2018. | Series: Game face
Summary: Alana O'Brien has just been nominated to represent her school at a STEAM Expo, but with seventh grade hockey tryouts and a family legacy to uphold, Alana will try any zany experiment she can think of to win the expo and give her an advantage of the ice.
Identifiers: LCCN 2017946553 | ISBN 9781532130465 (lib.bdg.) | ISBN 9781532131066 (ebook) | ISBN 9781532131363 (Read-to-me ebook)
Subjects: LCSH: Science fairs--Juvenile fiction. | Science--Experiments--Juvenile fiction. | Hockey--Juvenile fiction. | Self-reliance in adolescence--Juvenile fiction.
Classification: DDC [FIC]--dc23
LC record available at https://lccn.loc.gov/2017946553

TABLE OF CONTENTS

ONE

Science Whiz Kid

"Ah, is there anything better than a new robot?" I said happily.

It was Friday Exploration Day in the Makerspace. It was my favorite day in my favorite place. I was at the robotics table, programming a four-wheel rover to move through a maze of obstacles.

Rana was at the sewing machines, constructing something out of colorful fabric strips. Louie worked at the mixed medium table, building an old-fashioned volcano out of Play-Doh and a soda bottle. A few kids used laptops to design pieces of furniture, while others waited for their results at the 3-D printers.

Two years ago, an anonymous family donated the Makerspace, technology and all, to Cape

Elementary for its STEAM program. STEAM stands for science, technology, engineering, art, and math.

STEAM subjects are my favorites. Doc, our eighth-grade science teacher, happens to be my favorite teacher, too.

As we worked, Doc circled around the room, handing back lab reports. His eyes looked buggy behind the magnified lenses of his safety goggles.

"Remember to take notes as you work," he reminded us.

The Makerspace only had three rules:

1. Safety first!

2. Try, try again!

3. Always take notes!

He slid the lab report on my table. The red scribbly handwriting called my name from the corner of the page. I couldn't resist taking a peek.

98% Well done, as always! Small deduction for mislabeling Carbon (C, not CO!)

I smiled and clipped the paper into the correct section of my binder. Just then, the bell rang.

"Remember, class," Doc said as we quickly cleaned up our work stations. "In just two weeks, Cape Elementary has the honor of hosting the first ever Massachusetts STEAM Convention!"

My ears perked up. I had been waiting all summer for this. Students and teachers from across the state were coming to our Makerspace to spend the day working on exciting projects. There would be group competitions, hands-on experiments, and even a chance to work with professional scientists!

"I hope you're all ready to run on full STEAM!" Doc joked over the hustle and bustle. "Get it? STEAM?"

Rana and Louie met me at my table, their backpacks zipped and ready to go.

"Nice job with Vesuvius over there," joked Rana.

She poked Louie in the ribs.

"At least mine doesn't look like something from the lint drawer," Louie replied.

"Are you kidding?" said Rana, waving her fabric creation in the air. "This is clearly a fashionable tassel. They're everywhere this season. I'm just keeping up with the trends."

"Break it up you two," I said. "Both of your projects looked great."

"Easy for you to say, Alana," said Rana. "I bet you built that entire robot by hand during study hall, didn't you?"

My cheeks blushed slightly.

"You did!" said Louie. "The Science Whiz Kid strikes again!"

"Let's go," I said. "Maya's waiting for us in the cafeteria. It's mac and cheese day!"

Rana, Louie, Maya, and I had been best friends since kindergarten. We had lunch together every day at the same round table in the corner of the cafeteria. As we headed for the door, Doc tapped me on the shoulder.

"Can I speak with you for a moment, Alana?" he asked.

"Go ahead," I said to the girls. "Save me a seat."

There was a burnt hole in the elbow of Doc's white lab coat. I wondered how it got there.

"I'll get right to the point," said Doc, fidgeting with his pocket protector. "I am nominating you for the eighth-grade STEAM Expo!"

I nearly lost my balance and toppled over.

"Me?" I asked.

The STEAM Expo was a competition open only to eighth graders. It was the highlight of the STEAM Convention. Every school nominated one student to compete. When Doc told our class this, I hoped he would pick me. When I never heard anything, I figured he must have chosen someone else.

"Yes, you!" said Doc. "I'm sorry I couldn't tell you until now, but that's part of the rules. It was the only way to keep the playing field level. So, you'll do it?"

"I would be honored!" I answered.

"Eureka!" said Doc. "I think you have a real shot of winning. You are a gifted scientist, Alana O'Brien."

I beamed at the compliment.

"Your challenge is simple," he continued. "Take a tool and change its purpose. Pretty open ended, right? That's what makes it so hard. The possibilities are endless!"

My mind buzzed.

"Take a tool and change its purpose," I repeated. "Like turning an egg carton into a seed garden? Or using a potato to light a light bulb?"

"Exactly!" Doc answered.

"Can you help me with the project?" I asked.

Doc hesitated.

"Well," he said, "technically, I am allowed to offer guidance. But I cannot give any hints or specific suggestions. The judges are very strict. Just remember what you've learned about the engineering process and you'll be just fine."

Doc pointed to a poster on the wall. Large, black arrows circled clockwise around the words ASK, IMAGINE, PLAN, CREATE, IMPROVE and, finally, back to ASK.

"Now, off you go to lunch," he said. "A little birdie told me it's mac and cheese day!"

I floated down the halls to the cafeteria.

"You look happy!" said Louie as I plopped down into the empty seat next to her.

"Here," said Rana, "we got you an appetizer."

She handed me an overflowing plate of ooey, gooey mac and cheese. My stomach rumbled in thanks.

"You know me too well," I said, digging into my first bite.

As I plowed through the mound of macaroni, I told the girls my news.

"That's awesome!" said Louie. "So what tool are you going to change?"

"I'm not sure," I answered. "Thankfully, I don't have anything else going on next week and can spend some time tinkering in the Makerspace after school."

"Um," said Maya. "Aren't you forgetting something?"

She exchanged a sideways glance with Rana and Louie. I swirled my finger across the plate, wiping up the last bits of golden cheese sauce.

"What?" I asked, licking my lips.

"Ice hockey tryouts," answered Louie. "They start on Monday."

The sauce turned sour in my mouth.

"Oh no!" I said. "I completely forgot."

The following Monday afternoon, the locker room was packed. Even though it was only the end of September, girls were getting ready for winter sports tryouts. I felt a shiver of sadness, not ready for the cold months to hit. Fall was my favorite time of year on the Cape.

During summer, our salty seaside town turns into a tourist hot spot. When August ends, the streets clear out and the town becomes the sleepy community us year-round locals love so much.

But then winter hits. The brisk days are replaced by harsh winds. Even the grumpiest old men yearn for the humid summer crowds.

I had spent all weekend brainstorming for the STEAM Expo and had come up with a few possible ideas. My favorite so far was a birdhouse made out of different types of birdseed. It would allow birdwatchers to track which types of food was most popular as their feathered friends pecked away.

I needed time in the Makerspace to test out animal-friendly adhesives. But my schedule today had been packed with no free periods. Now, when I should typically have free time after school, ice hockey tryouts stood in my way.

"Remind me again why you don't think you'll make the team?" asked Rana.

"Are you joking?" I asked. "Look at me!"

I stuck out my arms and twirled in a circle to show off my barely five-foot-tall frame.

"I'm the smallest girl in our entire grade," I said. "I'll get crushed out there!"

"What about me?" asked Louie. "I'm small, but I'm not worried. We can't body check, remember? It's against the rules in girl's ice hockey."

"But you can still make contact as long as you're going for the puck," I said. "Besides, you're strong. I've got no muscles at all."

Louie was a competitive dancer in a group that did lots of acrobatic tumbling. She could do a handstand without blinking an eye. She could also probably pick me up without breaking a sweat.

"That's not true!" said Rana. "You have a huge brain!"

I smiled softly. Rana had an answer for everything.

"Actually," I said, "the brain is an organ, not a muscle. But I appreciate the compliment."

"You know what I mean," Rana said. "I don't get it. Why didn't you just tell your dad that you don't want to play?"

"It's not that I don't want to play," I explained, "because I really do. I just don't want my dad and brothers to be upset if I don't make the team. I'm the fourth and final kid. It's my duty to fulfill the family's frozen legacy. What if I can't?"

My family eats, sleeps, and dreams ice hockey. Mom died when I was a baby. So it's always been me and the boys. Growing up, I spent my winter weekends sipping hot chocolate in one rink or another. Dad is the head coach of the Cape's minor league men's ice hockey team, the Icebergs.

My three older brothers, Billy, Teddy, and Timmy, were all local ice hockey legends. Billy, the oldest, is now the starting right wing for his college's Division One team. Teddy helped Cape High win the national championship two years in a row as a defenseman. When Timmy joined the varsity team last year, he became the youngest starting goalie in the school's history.

I was laced into skates before I learned how to walk. I'm fast, and can pass the puck pretty well. Unfortunately, I missed out on the height gene.

I've always worried that I wouldn't be able to compete in a real game situation. I managed to avoid the issue since Cape Elementary girls' team didn't begin until eighth grade. Now, in my final year of middle school, the gig was up.

"You don't know if you don't try," said Louie. "So quit your pity party and suit up."

I let out a sigh, unzipped my bag, and started the long process of changing into my gear.

First, I slipped into my spandex tights. Next, I strapped kneepads around my legs and pulled heavy wool socks over them. Then, I shimmied into my girdle and black padded pants, tying them securely around my waist.

Before I moved to upper body, I stepped into my skates and tied the laces as tightly as possible.

"Lace up before waist up," I said. Dad taught me the rhyme years ago.

Shoulder pads, elbow pads, jersey, and neck guard followed. By the time I fixed my braids and shoved the caged helmet over my head, I had already broken a sweat.

"Here goes nothing," I mumbled through my mouth guard.

Knocked Down

My breath formed tiny white clouds in the frigid rink air. I stood like a statue near the boards. Girls skated before me in swirling patterns. A stream of glossy pucks glided over the shiny surface.

I looked around the hockey rink. On either end of the oblong ice rested the nets. A red line divided the rink in half. On either side of that, two blue lines mirrored one another, forming the neutral zone. Five black face-off circles dotted the rink, two in front of each goal and one at center ice.

A sharp whistle sounded and a tall woman skated off the bench.

"Ladies," she shouted, "to the goal line!"

I skated cautiously to the thin black line by the net, trying not to get bumped in the chaos. Lara skated up alongside me. She cut her blades into the ice and stopped dramatically, sending a spray of shavings into the air.

"Hey, Shortstack," she said. "I didn't know you were trying out!"

"Quit chirping," said Dottie as she stopped next to Lara. "Alana, ignore her."

Dottie and Lara were two of the oldest and coolest girls in our eighth grade class. They played on the same summer softball team with me, Rana, and Louie.

"Lara's always showing off," whispered Rana. "Remember that home run she hit last year? She's *still* talking about it. I'm taking off-season batting practice this year. I can't wait to give her a run for her money when the season starts again."

I smiled and turned my attention back to the woman at center ice.

"I'm Coach Riley," she said. "On the bench, we've got Assistant Coach Brady. Over the next two weeks, our goal is to build the strongest team possible. Unfortunately, that means we'll need to make some cuts to reach our final roster. Let's get started."

"I always heard she was tough," whispered Rana. "Turns out, she is."

Coach Riley pulled a slip of paper from her pocket and began reading names. When she got to me, she paused. "O'Brien?" she asked. "Is your dad the coach for the Icebergs?"

I nodded.

"Excellent!" she said. "Glad to see you've come out for the team."

"Great, more pressure," I muttered.

Coach Riley finished reading the names. Then she tucked the paper back into her pocket.

"We're going to work on footwork and conditioning today," she said. "Let's begin with a drill called Russian Circles. On my whistle, you'll start from the goal line and sprint to the other side of the rink, making your way around each face-off circle as you skate."

I sighed with relief. At least this first drill wouldn't involve battling another player.

"Louie, you're up first," Coach Riley said.

She blew her whistle. Louie took off as fast as she could. When she rounded the first circle, Coach Riley blew another sharp blast. The next skater began her drill.

As the line inched its way along the boards, the crunching sound of blades digging into ice filled the rink. Before I knew it, I was up.

"Go!" Coach Riley shouted. The whistle screeched in my ear.

I took a deep breath and pushed off. I skated quickly toward the first circle and concentrated on proper form. Knees bent. Shoulders back. Head up. Speed was important, but so was balance.

As I started to round the curve, I crossed one skate in front of the other. I staggered my strokes to generate speed and hug the curve at the same time. I sprinted toward the second circle on the opposite side of the zone, repeating the footwork as I swirled around the circular line. I finished the drill without falling once, proud of myself for a strong first showing.

"Nice work," Coach Riley said after everyone had taken their turn. "A strong player needs to be steady on their skates no matter which direction they are headed. So, for our second drill, you are going to do it again, but backwards."

She blew her whistle and we were off. I couldn't believe my luck. I could do this one, too!

When it was my turn, I spun around and positioned my skates shoulder width apart. I shuffled backward as if retreating from something in front of me. As I built up momentum, I used the crossover technique to move around the circles.

Up ahead, I noticed a player making C-cuts in the ice. She brought each skate out, away, and back to starting position. Dad taught me how to make C-cuts when I was little. It was a great technique to maintain your balance. At this level, Coach Riley would want something more advanced.

Pretty soon, I had completed two circles and was on my way to center ice. My confidence grew and I picked up speed. This was going better than expected!

I rounded the final curve, determined to stay upright. Just as I was about to finish the drill, my legs went out from under me. And suddenly, I was staring at the ceiling.

"Alana? Are you alright?" Coach Riley asked.

A bright light danced before my eyes. For a split second, I panicked. *Had something happened to my vision?* But then the light disappeared. It was just a flashlight. I popped out my mouth guard.

"Yes," I answered. "I think so."

I tried to prop myself up, but Coach Riley stopped me.

"Whoa, hold on a second, sport," she said. "That was some hit you took. Let's make sure you're safe first."

Coach Brady shined the flashlight in my eyes again. Then she asked me a few questions and checked my pulse. The entire team gathered around, gawking as I lay helpless on the freezing rink floor.

"Really," I said, "I feel fine. Can I get up now, please?"

Coach Brady extended her hand and helped me up. Coach Riley wiped some ice shavings off my shoulders.

"Girls," she continued. "This is a good learning experience. Beatrice, I appreciate the hustle, but you've got to be aware of your surroundings at all times. Even though it was an accident, if you plowed into someone like that during a game, you'd be thrown in the penalty box for an illegal body check."

Beatrice, a girl from my first period English class, was kneeling next to me on the ice.

"Sorry, Alana," she said. "Guess I need more practice skating backwards."

"No hard feelings," I answered. "I'm fine."

That was a lie. Even if my body felt fine, which it didn't, my ego was bruised. I had just gotten completely knocked down in front of most of the girls in the eighth grade. I ignored the stinging threat of tears and put on a brave face.

"Let's get back to drills," said Coach Riley. "Sprints are next. To the goal lines!"

As the rest of the girls lined up, Coach Brady knelt down to my eye level.

"Are you sure you're OK?" she asked. "I understand if you want to sit out for the rest of practice. That looked like it hurt."

If I wanted an excuse to leave early, this was it. I wanted to say yes, but knew that I couldn't. I wouldn't make the team. But I couldn't disappoint Dad even further by not finishing tryouts.

"I'll stay," I said.

Coach Riley smiled. "That's the spirit," she said. "Now, let's get that blood pumping!"

Back in the locker room, Rana collapsed on the bench, completely exhausted. "How are you still standing, Alana?" she asked, kicking off her skates. "You won almost every sprint! Seriously, you had to be the fastest skater out there."

"Yuck," said Louie. "Your feet stink!"

Maya walked in and sat on the bench next to Louie. Her blue journal was nestled under an arm. She reached into her thick bun and pulled out a pencil hidden in the curls.

"How did it go?" she asked. "It looked like you were working on footwork and conditioning, right? Can I get a comment? I'm writing an article about winter team tryouts."

Maya was a junior sports reporter for our local newspaper, *Cape Chronicle*. She was a human encyclopedia that knew everything about sports. But she was also an awesome writer.

"Here's a comment," Louie said. "Everyone here is going to make the team!"

"Not everyone." I sighed. "Did you see me hit the ground like a sack of potatoes?"

"You got knocked down!" Louie said. "That doesn't count."

"Plus," said Rana, "you got back up, didn't you?"

I rolled my eyes.

"As much as I'd love to relive that horrible moment," I said, "I have to go home and get my homework done. I need all of my study hall time tomorrow to test some ideas out in the Makerspace."

Beatrice struggled with her bag as she walked. "Sorry again, Alana," she said. "See you tomorrow!"

"Is it just me," Rana whispered, "or does she seem smaller?"

I took a second look. On the ice, Beatrice looked tall and intimidating. But now, without her gear, she appeared normal.

"It's probably just her shoulder pads," suggested Louie. "They can be deceiving."

I glanced at the stuffed equipment bag at my feet. Suddenly, something clicked.

"That's it!" I shouted. "Louie, you're a genius!"

The wheels in my mind churned faster, a new idea forming. "Are there still shoulder pads left at the store?" I asked.

Louie's parents owned Lin Lane, the Cape's only general store. They sold everything from beach chairs to dish soap, including sports equipment.

"I think so," answered Louie, confused. "Why?"

I reached for my backpack and pulled out the two $20 bills tucked in the front pocket. I had been planning to use this birthday money for some new engineering block sets. This was now more important.

"How many will this get me?" I asked, handing her the money.

"If you get the cheap stuff, probably three pairs," she answered.

"That should do the trick," I said. "I'll take three."

"Why?" asked Rana. "You already have a set that work just fine."

I zipped my bag shut and smiled.

"Meet me in the Makerspace tomorrow," I said. "I'll explain everything."

THREE

Family Dinner

Later that night, I squirted a giant blob of ketchup onto my hot dog and reached for a handful of barbecue chips.

"Save some for the rest of us," teased Timmy. He swiped the bowl of potato salad before I had a chance to scoop a third serving.

"Let her eat," said Dad. "She needs energy for tryouts!"

I crushed the chips onto my hot dog, wrinkled my nose at Timmy, and took a bite.

Dad insisted that we eat dinner as a family as often as possible. The menu usually consisted of hot dogs, pizza, or fried takeout from the Clam Strip. It was a far cry from gourmet, but that didn't matter one bit.

"Where does all that food go?" asked Teddy.

I washed the hot dog down with a swig of cold milk.

"My brain," I responded.

Teddy laughed. "Good answer," he said.

Dad dumped a spoonful of baked beans onto my plate. "Were your skates sharp enough?" he asked. "Remember, you get more power from digging your blades into the ice before pushing off, Alana."

"They were very sharp," I said.

"Did you pull your laces tight so your ankles stayed straight?" asked Timmy. "Nobody likes a bender."

"Super tight," I said, reaching for a hot dog.

They had been asking the same questions all night long. I was starting to have serious concerns about their short-term memory.

I knew I should tell them about my wipeout, but they would just over react. An anxious knot formed in the pit of my stomach. I was regretting that last hot dog.

"I'm sure the coaches were impressed with your footwork," said Dad.

I smiled, touched at the confidence he had in me. They would be so upset when I didn't make the team. The knot grew larger. I searched for a way out.

"Hey, remember that STEAM Convention I was telling you about?" I asked. "It's next Friday."

"Oh, right!" said Dad, clapping his hands together. "Any fun projects in the lineup?"

I appreciated Dad's enthusiasm. But I knew he was only asking for my benefit. I was the only one in the family really passionate about science. Well, sort of. Mom had been a scientist, too.

Mom had worked at a fancy lab in the city that researched ways to preserve water. That was how she and Dad met. She was trying to find ways to limit the amount of water needed for professional sports, like filling hockey rinks. They were introduced at a conference and then married a month later.

"She might not have melted the rink, but she sure did melt my heart," Dad said whenever he told that story.

Teddy walked over to the counter. He returned with a package of oatmeal raisin cookies. I took two and polished each one off in one bite.

"We'll be doing all sorts of fun stuff," I said. "Plus, there's this STEAM Expo for eighth graders. Doc nominated me to compete in it!"

"Nice!" said Timmy.

He reached across the table for a high five. Dad did the same. My worry knot untangled the tiniest bit. They seemed pretty excited about this news. Maybe, if I won the STEAM Expo, it would take away the sting of not making the ice hockey team.

"Can I be excused?" I asked. "I have an idea and need to do some brainstorming before bed."

Dad smiled and pushed his chair back from the table. "Of course," he said. "Good night, kiddo." He kissed me on the cheek. I hugged him and grabbed two cookies for the road.

"Alright boys," said Dad. "You're on dish duty."

As I walked down the upstairs hallway, I peeked into Billy's room. Even though this was his second year away at college, it still felt strange seeing his bed perfectly made night after night, evidence that he hadn't been home in weeks.

Billy and I have always had a special bond. Maybe it's because he's the oldest, but I feel like I can tell him anything. Sometimes, I ask him for advice before Dad or the girls.

As the sky outside turned from golden yellow to shimmery blue, a beam of light came through the window. It bounced off the hockey trophies on his shelf. I sighed, knowing I had big skates to fill.

Back in my room, I changed into pajamas, grabbed my science notebook, and pulled the shoulder pads from my equipment bag. Ginger, my orange tabby cat, lay curled up in the corner of the bed. She purred as I gave her a quick nuzzle. Then I nudged her to the side and slipped under the quilt.

"Let me ask you, Ginger," I said, rubbing her belly. "What tools do you need to play ice hockey? Skates? Yep. Helmet? Check. Shoulder pads. You betcha."

She yawned and flipped onto her back, stretching out to increase belly rub real estate.

"Now, what is the purpose of shoulder pads?" I asked.

Ginger licked her tiny paw and rubbed her eye, her cat nap now over.

"To protect the players, of course," I continued.

I thought of Beatrice and her difference in appearance on and off the ice.

"But could this tool have a different purpose?" I asked. "Yes! Yes, it could."

Ginger looked up at me, clearly not convinced.

"What if instead of protection, the purpose of shoulder pads was to make a player look physically bigger than they really are? You know, like a scare tactic? Instead of thin strips of foam, the pads could be bulky, like real muscles. Biceps. Triceps. What are some other ones?"

I opened my science notebook and wrote down *research upper body muscles.*

"I'll call them Mighty Muscles!" I said, jotting down the clever name on the next line.

I inspected my shoulder pads and scribbled the list of parts: *shoulder caps, chest piece, body cushion, arm pads, back panels, Velcro straps.* Then, I sketched a design and outlined my plan.

My initial hypothesis was that I could engineer a new set of shoulder pads by adding extra foam to the preexisting frame. I would bulk up muscular areas, which would hopefully give the look of an intimidating upper body beneath my jersey.

I turned on my bedside lamp. Then I dug around the drawer to find a measuring tape and Mom's calculator. Over the years, I had collected science tools and toys like microscopes, digital scales, graduated cylinders, and more.

Last year for Christmas, the boys made me a Makerspace kit called the STEAM Trunk. It was a metal toolbox. They filled it with all sorts of neat stuff for tinkering. Hand tools, duct tape, a hot glue gun, bungee cords, yarn, circuit boards, batteries, Play-Doh, copper wire, and bags full of plastic construction pieces.

My favorite tool of all was Mom's calculator. Dad gave it to me when I won the Cape Elementary Build-A-Bridge Competition. It had chipped plastic corners and was missing a few buttons. But to me, it was perfect. The framed picture on my bedside table and the calculator were a few of the mementos I had of Mom.

I snuggled back into bed. Then I measured the various parts of the shoulder pads, adding the numbers up and recording them in my notebook. Based on my calculations, I would need three sets of pads to make one prototype of Mighty Muscles.

Hopefully, Louie would deliver on her promise. If not, I might need to buy a few extra sets and take out a Lin Lane loan.

Soon, my eyes grew heavy with sleep. Ginger crawled across the quilt. She nudged me with her nose, the sign that she was ready to cuddle. I carefully placed everything on the floor and switched off the bedside lamp.

"Good night, Mom," I said, blowing her faded photo a kiss. "Who knows, Ginger? Maybe Mighty Muscles will even help me make the team."

Within seconds, I fell into a deep sleep. All thoughts of the Makerspace and hockey rink melted away.

FOUR

Mighty Muscles

"Does anyone have a snack?" I asked. "I'm starving. Veggie lasagna for lunch? Come on!" As we made our way into the Makerspace the next afternoon, Rana tossed me a granola bar.

Doc stood at his desk with a wobbly pile of textbooks spilling out of his arms. His glasses were balanced on the tip of his nose. They were threatening to fall off and add a new crack to the already battered lenses.

"Hello girls," he said. "Please make yourself at home. I just returned from the library. Nothing like robotics research to help you blow off steam. Get it? STEAM!"

He snorted and placed the pile of books on his desk.

"Do you think he has a book of bad jokes?" Maya whispered. "Or does he come up with them on the fly?"

"Do you mind if we do some work on my STEAM Expo project?" I asked Doc.

"Not at all!" he said. "I'll just be over here if you need anything."

Louie handed me a paper shopping bag. The Lin Lane logo was stamped on the front in sparkly gold letters. To my surprise, the bag contained not three, but four sets of shoulder pads.

"Four?" I asked. "Do I owe you extra?"

She shook her head.

"Nah," she said. "It's on the house. My parents insisted."

I smiled, knowing Louie had more to do with it than she would admit.

"So," said Maya, "what's the plan?"

I pulled the shoulder pads out of the bag and set them on the table. Then, I opened my notebook and showed them my prototype sketch of Mighty Muscles.

"Allow me to explain," I said. "The purpose of shoulder pads is to protect ice hockey players, right?"

The girls nodded.

"Today, we're going to give these protective pads a more powerful purpose," I said. "Introducing Mighty Muscles. An innovative new piece of hockey equipment that will add bulk to the tiniest of players and scare off the strongest frozen foes!"

I flexed my wimpy arms for added affect. Doc strolled over from his desk.

"Imaginative idea," he said, taking a closer look at my sketch. "Remember, take notes as you work. Now, I really shouldn't say much more."

He returned to his desk, but kept peeking over the top of the robotics manual. I could tell he was more interested in my project than anything written on the page.

"So, are Mighty Muscles for the STEAM Expo or for ice hockey tryouts?" asked Maya.

"Hopefully both," I said, "but that's off the record. The primary objective is the STEAM Expo. However, Mighty Muscles could help my chances on the ice. Two birds, one stone. Catch my drift?"

"Science Whiz Kid, you never cease to amaze!" said Rana.

"We'll need to work quickly to get this done," said Maya, reviewing the plans. "I am covering the varsity soccer game later. Plus, you girls need to be at tryouts in an hour."

I glanced at the clock. My muscles tensed with anxiety. "No time to waste. Trapezius, deltoid, pectoral, biceps," I said, pointing to the various parts of the shoulder pads. "Now, watch closely."

I took a new set of pads, reached for a pair of scissors, and cut out a circular chunk of the foam. Then, I grabbed a needle and some black nylon thread. I sewed the foam onto the lowest part of the arm pad, underneath the plastic flap.

When I finished sewing, I lowered the flap back into place and compared the two arms.

"See?" I said, pointing out the difference. "This arm now has a larger bicep muscle!"

"Sweet!" said Louie. "It's like doing a month's worth of roundoffs in sixty seconds."

"Totally," joked Rana.

"Let's create an assembly line to finish this," I said. "Rana, can you please cut lengths of thread? Louie, you're in charge of cutting the foam. Maya and I will sew the new muscles onto the frame. Try your best to make it look like the sketch."

"You got it," Louie said, ripping into the pads.

"Maya," I said, "make sure we sew tightly enough to secure the foam to the frame."

"On it," she responded. "The last thing you need is a runaway tricep."

"What about me?" asked Rana. "Any important thread directions?"

"You're the fashion expert!" I laughed. "Go with your gut."

We moved quickly, each manning our task as we bulked up the Mighty Muscles. I kept my eye on each step of the process, taking notes as we worked. When the last piece of thread was knotted and nipped, I looked up at the clock.

"Just in time!" I said. "We have to hustle."

We quickly cleaned up our workstation and said goodbye to Doc. "Let me know how it goes!" he called as we ran out of the room.

After a world record sprint to the locker room, I hoisted the Mighty Muscles over my head and fastened them into place. Then I threw on the rest of my gear, laced up my skates, and sprinted to the rink.

It wasn't until I got on the ice that I noticed something was terribly wrong.

FIVE

Hulk on Skates

"You look like the Incredible Hulk!" joked Louie.

We were skating around the neutral zone. The cold rink air turned our breath to milky white curlicues. I tried my best to act normal despite curious looks from the other girls.

"Seriously," Louie continued. "I've seen gymnastic coaches less jacked than you!"

The Mighty Muscles prototype had several flaws. First, I should have determined exactly how big each muscle should be. Since I didn't, Louie cut each chunk of foam much larger than necessary.

Second, I didn't map out exactly where the foam needed to be sewn onto the frame. It turned out Maya and I had different ideas of where upper body muscles were located. As a result, the left bicep was higher than the right. One side of the chest was upside down. And the shoulders were mismatched. I looked like a mutant monster with strange bulges pulling at my jersey.

"Well, you wanted to scare away your opponents," Rana said. "You sure look scary in that getup!"

The piercing shriek of Coach Riley's whistle echoed across the rink.

"Goal lines!" she shouted.

"She's really not one for small talk, huh?" said Rana.

I skated toward the net. I hoped Coach Riley wouldn't notice my strange appearance.

"I saw a lot of potential and hard work yesterday," she began. "Let's keep up that energy today. We're going to begin with stick work."

Coach Brady set up a line of orange cones down the center of the rink.

"Puck control is crucial in ice hockey," Coach Riley said. "For our first drill, you're going to weave the stick handle in and out of these cones, bringing the puck with you. Let's quickly review proper form."

She held her hockey stick out in front of her body.

"The top hand of your grip provides all of the control," she said. "So make sure that is your dominant hand. I'm a righty, so I have a righty stick. See? The blade curves slightly this way. If you think you have the wrong stick, let me know and we'll take a look."

She gripped her hands around the stick, right on top of left.

"There are two types of strokes to keep in mind, forehand and backhand," she continued. "If you're a righty, forehand starts on the right side of the body. If you're a lefty, it starts on the left. Control the puck by cradling it on the face of your blade between the heel and the toe, and move the stick across your body. To bring the puck back, use the other side of the blade to stop it and tap back. Like so."

She demonstrated each stroke, pushing and pulling the puck back and forth.

"Now, you try," she instructed.

As soon as I started, it became clear that the Mighty Muscles were going to cause even more problems than just looking silly. The bulky foam limited my mobility and I couldn't bring my arms across my body like I needed to.

The puck escaped my reach before I had a chance to stop it. I regained control and tried again, hoping the pads just needed to settle into place. For the second time, I lost control of the puck.

My heart raced. I had to get these pads off now!

"Let's get started," Coach Riley said. "O'Brien. Why don't you start us off?"

My stomach dropped.

"You've got to be kidding me," I muttered under my breath.

I skated nervously to the first cone. Sweat dripped down the back of my neck. The rink was silent as the other girls watched and waited.

"Ready?" Coach Riley asked.

She held my eye for an extra beat and I could tell she knew something was off. Determined not to let her see me sweat, I tried my best to look confident. "Ready," I answered.

She chuckled and lifted the whistle to her mouth. "Go!" she shouted.

I struggled instantly and lost the puck around the first cone. I had to find a solution to this problem as quickly as possible. I scanned the line of cones and estimated the distance between each turn.

Traditional stick work was not an option. The most logical solution was to use speed. I took a

deep breath, regrouped, and started again. This time, after pushing the puck forward, I sprinted after it and tapped it around the next cone rather than use backhand. It was clunky, but effective. I managed to zigzag my way to the end of the line.

"Can I run to the bathroom for a sec?" I asked Coach Brady on the far side of the rink. "Too much lemonade at lunch."

Back in the locker room, I ripped off the Mighty Muscles. I tossed them in my bag, annoyed at their mere existence. Thankfully, I had packed the extra set of shoulder pads. I changed and hustled back to the ice in time for our first water break.

"What happened to the Hulk?" Louie asked.

She gave my arm a playful pinch. I slurped the water, eager to wash away the sting of failure.

"He's gone," I said. "Just like my chances of making the team. Did you see me out there? I was like a hunchback shuffling around. What's really frustrating is that I could have done that drill."

Coach Riley skated to the neutral zone. Then she blew her whistle.

"Does she ever relax?" groaned Rana.

"Time for positions," said Coach Riley. "Who knows what this area is called?"

Lara's hand shot up into the air. "Center!"

"Yes," said Coach Riley.

"What about here?" She skated to the right of the circle along the red line.

"Right wing," shouted Louie.

"Good," said Coach Riley.

She crossed the center circle and stopped on the same spot on the left side. "Here?" she asked.

"Left wing!" answered Beatrice.

Next, Coach Riley skated to the circles behind the blue line.

"Two defensemen are positioned here and here," she continued. "Hopefully, I don't need to show you where the goalie goes. Now, we're going to have a scrimmage and give you a chance to try a few positions."

I kicked myself for the Mighty Muscle mistakes. This is exactly what I needed them for! Coach Riley started selecting the teams.

"Rana," she said, "I heard you're a softball catcher. Is that right?"

"Yes!" Rana answered. "I've been playing since I was a little kid."

"Excellent," said Coach Riley. "Throw on some goalie pads and head to the net."

Next, she looked at me. "O'Brien, let's start you at center. Get ready for your first face-off."

I chewed nervously on my mouth guard and skated to center circle. Just my luck, Beatrice waited for me on the other side. My back hurt just thinking of yesterday's wipeout.

"Keep your sticks steady until the puck drops," said Coach Riley. "Remember, you've each got two wingers waiting for the pass."

To my right, Louie had her stick low and ready to strike. To my left, Dottie smiled reassuringly. If I could just pass to one of them, maybe I could get out of this unharmed.

Coach Riley held the puck high in the air. Beatrice and I lowered our sticks. My heart pounded. The whistle blew.

"Go!" she shouted.

In her eagerness, Beatrice lurched forward and lost her balance. Right before she toppled onto the ice, I got my stick to the puck, tapped it to Louie, and escaped her falling frame. Louie caught the pass and sprinted forward.

I moved nimbly around Beatrice as she struggled to get back on her skates. Lara loomed as a defenseman for the other team, ready to stop our attack.

As we approached the blue line, I watched Louie, knowing I couldn't enter the offensive zone before the puck. If I did, our team would get a penalty for being offside. Then we'd have to face off again, something I really didn't want to do.

Louie charged across the blue line, skating fearlessly toward the net. Lara stepped up to block her. Louie shot the puck toward the corner boards, slingshotting it behind the goal toward the other side of the zone.

Dottie hustled to receive the pass. But the other defenseman got there first and broke up the play. Thankfully, our two defensemen were waiting at the blue line and stopped the puck from breaking the neutral zone.

"Excellent work!" shouted Coach Riley. "Keep the play alive!"

Our defender passed the puck back to Dottie. I hovered near the top of the zone, hoping that Louie could break open for another pass. Unfortunately,

Lara now had her trapped against the boards. Dottie turned to me.

"Alana!" she shouted. "Coming to you!"

Dottie sent the puck flying across the ice, but it ricocheted off the blade of a nearby skate. I sprinted to the boards and regained control just as Beatrice started to charge. I backpedaled, protecting the puck and looking for a way out.

A memory popped into my head. Last year, Doc took our science class on a field trip to see Cape High's new pool table in the student lounge. We spent the trip hitting cue balls off of the bumpers as Doc taught us about velocity and angles.

I looked at the boards and knew exactly what to do. I pivoted my body forty-five degrees and shot the puck straight into the wall. Then, I dodged left. Beatrice lunged forward and missed me completely.

At the same time, the puck hit the boards precisely as I hoped it would and bounced back to my stick. I caught it, squared my hips, and faced the goal. I aimed for the upper left corner of the net and delivered a wrist shot. The puck sailed past the goalie and swished against the empty net.

"Goal!" I shouted, unable to contain my excitement.

Coach Riley blew her whistle and stopped play.

"Nice one!" cheered Louie.

"Creative thinking, O'Brien," said Coach Riley. "And a nice shot to boot. OK, you three, let's switch up offensive lines and give someone else a try."

I began to make my way off the ice with Dottie and Louie. My heart was still pounding with joy. It was just the boost in confidence I needed.

"On second thought," called Coach Riley, "you two, stay here. O'Brien, hit the bench."

The smile fell from my face as I watched the next group of players slide onto the ice. Their bodies blurred together into a teary haze.

SIX

Clear Your Mind

The next few days passed in a frustrating blur. I spent every spare second thinking of ways to improve Mighty Muscles. But nothing seemed right.

In the meantime, practices continued. And I still hadn't found a way to make myself stand out from the group. My next free period came around on Wednesday afternoon. So I went to Doc in search of guidance.

"These were a bust," I said, tossing the failed Mighty Muscles on the table. I told him everything. When I was finished, I looked up, eager for his advice.

"You had a minor setback, Alana," he said. "That's supposed to happen! If everything worked out on the first try, nobody would need to study STEAM. But you can't just give up. Now, what's the next step in the engineering process?"

I glanced up at the poster. "Improve," I said.

"Eureka!" he said. "Improve! We must always be asking ourselves, 'What can I do to improve this design?' So, what do you think?"

I noticed a smudge of suspicious green sludge on the bottom of Doc's lab coat and wondered how it got there. I sighed.

"That's just it," I answered. "I don't think there's anything I can do to improve Mighty Muscles. I've been brainstorming all week. And I've realized that there is a very critical flaw in my idea."

"What's that?" he asked.

"Well, the whole idea behind Mighty Muscles was to bulk me up," I began. "That might make me look more intimidating on the ice. But it will also make it impossible for me to move my arms. I'm so little to begin with. I ran the numbers. Even if I decreased the size of the foam by half, it still gets in the way."

Doc thought quietly for a few minutes, looking over my notes.

"Hmm," he finally said. "You might be right. I'm no ice hockey expert, but moving your arms is pretty important, right?"

"Unfortunately," I answered glumly.

Doc reached over and snapped my notebook shut. I looked at him, surprised.

"Well, a good engineer also knows when its time to move on," he said. He stood up and stretched. "Do you know what you need to do?"

"What?" I asked.

"Stop thinking about Mighty Muscles," he answered. "When you clear your mind, you allow inspiration to enter."

"That's it?" I asked. "That's all the advice I get?"

"I'm afraid so," he answered. "Remember the rules! Now, go spend some time with your friends.

But keep your notebook with you. You never know when an idea will hit!"

Later that week, on Friday night, I met the girls at Pete's, the Cape's best pizzeria. We sat around my favorite booth. Timmy and some guys from the hockey team sat nearby.

During summer, it was impossible to get a table without waiting at least forty-five minutes. But I liked eating at Pete's in the off-season. The red and white checkered tablecloths made the room feel warm, and the soft glow of candlelight filled the space with a sparkly gold haze.

"Can I have the last piece?" I asked. "I need to drown my sorrows in cheese."

Louie handed me the thick slice with crispy air bubbles in the center. I peeled off each greasy slab of pepperoni. Then I stacked them on top of one another before popping them in my mouth.

"That really was the leaning tower of pizza!" joked Maya. "Get it?"

I bit into the salty crust. "You're such a word nerd," I said with a laugh, crumbs spilling from my lips. "No wonder you're the busiest sports reporter in town."

"Finally! A smile," she said. "I was starting to think we'd lost you."

I wiped my fingers on the front of my shirt, leaving behind a trail of grease. "Sorry," I said. "I've been in a bad mood all night, haven't I?"

"I don't know why you're upset," said Rana. She slurped up a string of spaghetti. "Tryouts are going well!"

"Maybe for you guys," I answered, "but Coach Riley hasn't played me at center since our first practice. She never puts me in at defense. And I can't remember the last time she asked me to start a drill. That's not a good sign."

"Remember the look on your dad's face when you told him about your goal?" said Maya, trying to make me feel better. "He was so happy!"

I sighed. "Don't you see? That makes it even worse. Now his hopes are even higher that I'll make the team. On top of it all, the STEAM Expo is one week away. I still have no idea what to make."

I looked at my notebook on the red vinyl booth next to me. We'd been trying to come up with ideas all night. So far, all I had written down were crazy contraptions. *Night vision helmet. Glow in the dark mouth guard. Magnetic puck.*

"What about skate stilts?" asked Rana. "You know, like the kind circus clowns wear? We could add fabric to your hockey pants to cover them up!"

I considered the idea. "I like your enthusiasm," I said. "But it's hard enough balancing on thin blades. If you add height to the equation, gravity would take over and bring me down."

"If Louie can balance on that tiny beam, I bet you can balance on some skate stilts," she answered. "You can give her some pointers, right?"

"Maybe," answered Louie, "but people might also have a hard time believing that the shortest girl in the grade somehow grew a foot overnight."

"Minor detail," said Rana.

We sat in silence for a few minutes as the waitress cleared the piles of greasy napkins and sauce-stained plates.

"Well, girls," said Maya, "what we have here is a case of writer's block. Take it from a pro. This could last a while. There's only one thing to do to get the creative juices flowing."

I looked up hopefully. "What?" I asked.

She smiled. "Ice cream!" she said.

It was the best idea I had heard all night.

"Good thinking!" I said. "Come on. Timmy can drive us to the Scoop on the way home. He still gets an employee discount in the off-season."

Timmy had worked behind the ice cream counter at the Scoop for the past two summers. During the busy months, when the line snaked out the door and down the block, he always treated us to free toppings.

"Let's go," I said. My worries were replaced by the promise of chocolate chip cookie dough.

As we piled into the back seat of the station wagon, Timmy tossed a canvas bag in the trunk. Metal clanged against metal as the bag rolled to a stop.

"What's in there?" I asked.

Timmy clicked his seat belt into place and started the engine.

"Just a bunch of old skates from the guys on the team," he said. "We're donating them to charity. I wanted to see if the Icebergs' equipment manager could sharpen them. Some of the guys brought in skates from when they were little kids. I swear, the kiddie blades are half the size of what they wear now."

As he flipped on the bright headlights, a second light bulb flashed in my brain.

SEVEN

Extend-O Blades

"Extend-O Blades?" asked Maya. "I don't get it."

We were back in the Makerspace on Monday. Doc was perched at his desk, pretending to read a textbook while secretly eavesdropping.

"Timmy's bag of skates made me think," I explained. "When you get bigger, you outgrow your skates and get new ones, right? The bigger your skates, the longer your blades. Do you know what my problem is?"

"Where do I begin?" joked Louie.

I ignored her. "I haven't grown an inch since I was ten! That's almost three years ago! I'm still wearing the skates I had as a kid. Look at Lara. Her skates are much larger than mine. And much longer blades. It's got to be an advantage, right?"

Rana bit her lip and considered the idea. "You might be on to something," she admitted. "I get a new softball bat about every two years after I've grown a few more inches."

"Exactly. You can't cover the plate with a tiny bat," I said, pulling the skates out of my bag. I had attached plastic pieces from my STEAM kit to show the girls my design. "The traditional purpose of a skate blade is mobility, right? What if we changed the purpose? What if, instead of mobility, the blade

leveled the playing field for skaters of various sizes? My hypothesis is that adding length to my blade will increase my power, which takes away the advantage of a player much larger than me."

"What an innovative idea," said Doc, jumping up from his chair. "Well done!" He blushed, realizing he had said too much. "But don't tell the judges I said so," he added, returning to his seat.

"How are we going to build these newfangled blades?" asked Maya. She eyed my sketch.

I unplugged a laptop from the nearby charging station and clicked it to life. The machine slowly hummed as if waking up from a long nap.

"We're going to use the 3-D printers," I said.

The girls huddled around the laptop. I opened up the software program and glanced at the clock. Once again, we didn't have much time.

"This design program is user friendly," I began. "It lets you draw simple shapes, then turn them into 3-D structures. A box, for example, starts out as a rectangle. A cylinder starts as a circle. See?"

I opened a new document. Then I selected the rectangle icon from the toolbar.

"Now," I explained, "switch to Push-Pull mode and adjust, like so." I clicked the center of the rectangle and moved the mouse up. Magically, the flat rectangle grew into a 3-D box with shaded sides to show dimension and depth.

"See!" I said. "Now we have a box."

"Cool!" whispered Rana. "I really need to start paying more attention in class."

"I heard that," said Doc.

I pulled Mom's calculator and the tape measure out of my backpack.

"Over the weekend," I continued, "I measured the length of Timmy's skate blade. He is a size thirteen, which gives him a blade that's fourteen inches long. Then, I measured my skates, which are a junior size six. My blade is seven inches long. That's a difference of seven inches between our blades. I know what you're thinking. Adding seven inches to my blade might limit my turning radius."

"That's *exactly* what I was thinking," Maya joked.

"Thankfully, the math isn't too complicated," I continued. "Timmy is approximately two feet taller than me. The tallest girl at tryouts is Lara. I estimate her to be one foot taller than me. One foot is half of two feet, right? So all I need to do is take the difference between my blade and Timmy's blade and cut it in half. What is half of seven inches?"

"I know!" said Rana. "Three-and-a-half inches!"

"Yes!" I said, excited that they were catching on. "Three-and-a-half extra inches is all I need."

"So," said Louie, "we need to build a blade that's three-and-a-half inches?"

I erased the box on the screen and refreshed the page. "That was my original plan," I explained, "but then I remembered how bulky the Mighty Muscles turned out."

"That's why you always take notes," said Doc. He had abandoned his book and was now standing by my side. A trail of purple spots were on his lab coat collar. I wondered how they got there.

"See?" he said. "You learned something from Mighty Muscles after all."

I nodded.

"The 3-D printer creates shapes using a plastic polymer, which can be bulky in large quantities," I continued. "I think it will be safer to cut the design in half. We print two extensions that are each 1.75 inches long. In my mind, they look like this."

To create the base of the blade, I started with a rectangle and pulled it into a box. Then, I drew a line down the top of the box and pulled it up, creating a pointed roof.

"This part will actually be on the bottom. See? If you flip it over, it becomes the pointed edge of the blade," I explained.

To create a space for my existing blade, I drew a small circle in the center of the box's side. Then, I pushed the circle in, making a slit in the surface.

"It's a simple design," I said. "If my calculations are correct, this will fit snugly on my blade, be sharp enough to cut through the ice, and give me the power of someone much taller. I don't want to jinx it, but I'm amazed at how easy that was!"

I looked up from the screen. The girls stared silently back at me. "What?" I asked.

"Easy?" joked Louie. "Honestly, you scare us sometimes, you know that?"

I laughed and clicked print. The 3-D printer in the corner of the room buzzed to life. Its mechanical arm moved back and forth, filling the air with a rhythmic whooshing sound.

"This will take several hours to print, Alana," said Doc. "They probably won't be ready until tomorrow morning."

"Yikes," said Maya. "That's cutting it pretty close, don't you think?"

"I'll say," I said, gulping nervously. "Our last tryouts are tomorrow. And the STEAM Expo is in just four days. Close is an understatement."

Suddenly, the bell rang.

"I'll keep an eye on them," said Doc. "Stop by first thing tomorrow morning to get your results!"

EIGHT

Red vs. Blue

"Welcome to the final day of ice hockey tryouts," said Coach Riley.

It was the following afternoon, and we were lined up on the goal lines. Only one practice left to impress the coaches.

I had barely slept a wink last night, worried about what would be waiting for me in the Makerspace this morning. Thankfully, the Extend-O Blades had turned out quite nicely!

"These look wonderful," Doc had said, handing me the finished product.

Just as I had planned, the four white, rectangular bases came together in a perfectly pointed edge. I turned each plastic piece over to find the thin slit running along the center.

"Moment of truth," I said as I grabbed a skate from my equipment bag.

Carefully, I wedged one piece of plastic on the front end of my blade. The shiny metal of the skate fit snuggly into place. I exhaled a sigh of relief. Next, I added the second piece of plastic on to the back end of the skate. Again, the pieces fit together perfectly. I turned the skate around in my hand, admiring the longer blade.

"Check it out," I said. "It worked!"

Doc gave me a high five. "Don't tell the judges about that, either." He winked.

Now, as I waited on the goal line, I shuffled my skates back and forth. I watched the pointed plastic edge of the Extend-O Blades cut sparkly grooves in the ice.

"Today," Coach Riley continued, "we are going to work on communication and teamwork. Let's play a little game. Everyone on the right side of the net is one team. Everyone to the left is another."

Coach Brady handed out red and blue jerseys to the different teams. As I pulled the blue jersey over my head, I thought of the failed Mighty Muscles. And I hoped my second idea would work better.

"Here's how it works," explained Coach Riley. "Red team starts at right wing facing forward. Blue team starts at left wing, facing the opposite direction. On the sound of my whistle, everyone skates along the boards. If you are passed by someone from the opposite team, hit the bench because you're out. Whichever team runs out of players first, loses. Ready? Get in position."

As my team assembled along the red line, I realized that the directions were too simple. There had to be more strategy to it.

"Listen up," I whispered to my team. "This is about communication, right? Make sure you warn someone if they are about to get passed. Some of us will be able to last longer than others, and that's OK. We can use that to our advantage. We'll work together to keep certain skaters on the ice for the final push."

I felt confident. This was a puzzle, and I was good at puzzles. I scanned the other team's lineup.

"Lara and Louie are their strongest skaters," I whispered. "They will lead the attack."

Beatrice leaned heavily on her stick, her head hanging limp.

"I don't feel so good," she said.

Even through her helmet cage, I could see her face turning a green hue. She would be an easy target. I surveyed the rest of our options. Rana was a good skater, but speed wasn't really her specialty. She would get passed early on, as well.

"Beatrice, hold on as long as you can," I said. "Even if they pass you, tire them out in the process."

I did some quick mental math, knowing that was a factor, too.

"In order to win, we'll need to have a strategy. Our goal is to knock out two of their players for every one of ours," I explained. "We should all try to separate ourselves from one another. That way, if they pass one of us, at least they only knock out one, not two. Make sense? Dottie, let's set a fast pace and make some early moves."

Dottie shook her head in agreement. Before I had a chance to review the game plan, Coach Riley blew her whistle and we were off.

Dottie kept pace with me as we rounded the first corner. I saw Lara and Louie do the same on their side. The crunching of skates filled the air. Within seconds, Dottie and I made it to the opposite side of the neutral zone. I checked over my shoulder as Lara started her attack on Beatrice.

"Beatrice!" I shouted. "Speed up!"

Beatrice heard my direction. She skated out of Lara's reach long enough to give Dottie time to pass two of the red team's skaters in front of us.

"You're out!" Coach Riley said, making sure the passed players made it safely to the bench. "Beatrice, you, too!"

I stayed alert, warning my teammates of potential passes or calling out directions to girls who showed signs of fatigue. As we sprinted around the boards, the rink quickly turned into a sea of jagged blade cuts.

I closed in on two of the red team's skaters. Just as I was about to pass, I noticed Louie gaining ground on Rana on the other end of the rink.

"Rana," I shouted, "hustle up. Try to get past the goal line!"

She heard me and raced out of harm's way. At the same time, I sped up and whizzed by the two tired skaters in my path. Coach Riley's whistle blew, signaling another loss for the red team.

After several minutes, the only skaters that remained were me, Dottie, Lara, and Louie. Just as I suspected from my initial observation.

Teammates cheered us on from the bench as we skated around the rink, lap after lap in a never-ending loop.

"Alana! Watch out!" Dottie shouted.

She was a few feet in front of me, but had turned around just in time to issue the warning.

I sensed movement close behind and knew someone was on my heels. I sped up slightly, not wanting to get too close to Dottie and risk us both getting knocked out at the same time.

The noise behind me faded, and for a second, I thought I was in the clear. But as I crossed the red line, my skate got caught in a deep groove. The Extend-O Blades ripped off, causing me to lose my balance and fall.

My arms went out in front of me as I slid across the ice. Unable to stop, I crashed directly into the back of Dottie's skates and dragged her down in a tangled heap. Louie, who had been on my heels the whole time, breezed past us.

Coach Riley blew the whistle.

"Game over!" she announced. "Red team wins!"

I sighed as the rest of the girls returned to the ice. They carried their sticks.

I rolled off of Dottie, giving in to the exhaustion that spread through my limbs. A cold shiver swept across me as I lay motionless. Losing the drill for my team was bad, but adding a second wipeout to my resume was even worse.

"Nice race, Alana," said Dottie. She brushed the ice from her knee pads as we got up.

"Sorry for the hit," I muttered.

"Don't sweat it." She winked. "Here, I think these belong to you."

She handed me the broken pieces of Extend-O Blades and skated off to the bench for a water break. I shoved the cracked plastic into my pockets and followed her, my head hanging low.

"Nice job, today," Coach Riley said at the end of practice. She smiled as we gathered around center circle. "You've all worked really hard and should be proud of yourselves. If I could take all of you on the team, I would."

I avoided her gaze but could sense her looking at me. Surely, she was trying to soften the blow.

"I know how hard it can be to wait for the news," she said. "Which is why we plan to call you all tonight with our final decision."

My jaw tightened. Tonight? I didn't expect them to have an answer so soon.

Back in the locker room, I dropped my head between my hands, unable to find the energy to change out of my gear. I pulled the Extend-O Blades from my pockets and assessed the damage.

"You still have two days to figure this out," said Louie, patting me on the back.

"Remember what Doc said," added Rana. "Improve! Improve! Improve! These worked so well before the ice got bumpy. All they need is a little tweaking and they could be just right! Don't give up."

I sighed.

"You saw me out there today," I said. "There's no way I'm making the team now. And if I don't figure out how to fix these blades, I don't stand a chance of winning the STEAM Expo either."

NINE

Brotherly Advice

For a split second, I thought I was seeing a ghost. There, leaning up against our station wagon in the parking lot after practice, was Billy! He was holding a pink polka-dotted box from Sweet Baby Jane's, my favorite bakery.

"Billy!" I said, dropping my hockey bag. "What are you doing here?"

I jumped into his arms. He twirled me twice, then set me down carefully on two feet.

"I arranged my class schedule so that I could take a few days off," he said. "I wanted to hear all about your ice hockey tryouts. I brought cupcakes to celebrate. Red velvet. Your favorite!"

He lifted the lid of the delicate pastry box. Two perfectly whipped dollops of frosting stared back at me. It was such a kind gesture. Suddenly, I couldn't hold back any longer and the tears started to flow.

"What's wrong? I thought you liked red velvet."

There, it all came pouring out. I told Billy everything, from how I'd messed up during tryouts, to not wanting to disappoint Dad, to my troubles with the STEAM Expo.

Finally, when there were no words left, I wiped my eyes and waited for his response.

"We're going to need something stronger than cupcakes," he said.

The warm golden sand of Lambert's Beach was completely uncluttered this time of year.

During the summer, families arrive at the crack of dawn to get their umbrellas set up along the water. There's never enough room to put down more than one or two beach towels.

And it's never quiet enough to sit and enjoy a good book. Always eager for batting practice,

Home Run Derby was Rana's favorite beach game. I couldn't count how many times I'd been smacked in the head with a whiffle ball. But on this late September afternoon, the beach was calm and clear.

"This should do the trick," said Billy.

He handed me a frothy root beer float from the Clam Strip, located on the other side of the grassy dunes. I swirled the straw around in the vanilla foam and watched a ribbon of root beer break the surface.

"Thanks," I said, taking a sip. "This really does hit the spot."

Billy leaned back against the picnic table and kicked off his sneakers. I did the same, burying my toes in the sun-dappled sand. We sat in silence for a while, sipping our floats as the waves lapped against the shore.

I noticed something sparkle a few feet up the strandline. I placed my cup down and walked over to the mystery object. Upon further inspection, I realized it was a copper penny. I picked it up and rubbed my finger along the smooth edges. Its ridges were worn away by years of erosion.

"Heads up," said Billy. "That's good luck."

Standing next to him, I remembered just how tall he was. On my tiptoes, I came up to about his belly button. I tucked the penny in my pocket and looked out at the horizon. The sun was falling fast, its beams kissing the spot where water meets sky.

"Did I ever tell you about the time I wanted to quit my hockey team?" Billy asked.

I looked up at him, shocked.

"What are you talking about?" I asked.

"I was in tenth grade," he explained. "Cape High had our first shot of winning the state championships. Our schedule was crazy with two-a-day practices, plus strength and conditioning sessions, and weekend games. I was getting a lot of playing time, and really liked the team dynamic. But I started to worry that I wasn't good enough for the added pressure. So, one afternoon, I made up some lame excuse about wanting to spend more time with my friends and asked Dad if I could quit. Want to know what he said?"

I nodded, unable to imagine how disappointed Dad must have been.

"He said 'Billy, I just want you to be happy, and if that means giving up ice hockey, then so be it,'" he answered.

My jaw dropped.

"What?" I asked, dumbfounded.

Billy laughed and nudged me in the ribs.

"Come on," he said. "Don't look so shocked, Alana Bridget O'Brien. Can you ever think of a time when Dad made us do something we didn't want to?"

I mulled it over a second. "No," I admitted.

"No," said Billy, "because he hasn't. Sure, he gives suggestions, but at the end of the day, he just wants us to be happy. He loves hockey and would be thrilled to see you make the team. If you don't, the only reason he'd be upset is if *you* were. He would do everything to help you practice and improve for next year's tryouts. But only if you *wanted* to. He loves you. We all do."

It was all I needed to hear. I threw my arms around Billy and held on for dear life as the salt water tickled our toes. The warm breeze wrapped around us, blowing away the stress from the past few days.

"So why didn't you quit the team?" I finally asked, curious to hear the end of the story.

Billy smiled.

"Well," he said, "the second thing Dad said was this. 'Billy, you are stronger than you can possibly imagine. When life gets tricky, the easy way out is to give up and doubt. Believing in yourself can be hard, but you can do it, and you'll always have me cheering you on from the sidelines.'"

He knelt down so that we were eye level.

"Believing in yourself can be hard," he repeated, "but you can do it, and you'll always have me cheering you on from the sidelines."

I hugged him again.

"That's better," he said. "See? Sometimes all you need is a big brother. I'm like one of those safety bars on a roller coaster. You hardly notice it when you get on. But it's the only thing keeping you from falling off when the ride gets bumpy."

The tingling of a new idea buzzed at the base of my neck.

"Billy," I said, "you're amazing! A safety bar. Why didn't I think of that?"

"Huh?" he asked.

"No time to waste!" I ran to the car. "Let's go, Billy!"

On our drive home, I explained my idea to Billy. All the Extend-O Blades needed was some type of safety device. A separate clip or a flexible latch that looped around the metal blade to keep the plastic in place.

"I just need to figure out what design will work best," I said as we pulled into the driveway. "Thankfully, I have one more study hall tomorrow morning. It will be close, but I might just be able to try this one more time."

Dad scooped me up in a bear hug the second we walked in the door.

"Special delivery, huh?" he said, winking at Billy. "What did I ever do to deserve such great kids like you?"

"Funny," I said, Billy's words still fresh in my mind. "I was thinking the same thing about you!"

Just then, the phone rang.

"That's for me," I said. "Be right back."

I ran into the den and settled down onto the couch. I took a deep breath before picking up the receiver. I knew it would be Coach Riley.

This was it. The moment of truth.

I felt a sense of calm wash over me. Whatever the outcome, I would still have a loving family waiting for me to hear the news.

"Hello?" I said.

"O'Brien? This is Coach Riley," she said in her now familiarly gruff tone. "How are you?"

"Great!" I said. For the first time this week, I really was.

"I'll get right to the point," she said. "I wanted to thank you for your hustle this week and let you know that Coach Brady and I have thought long and hard about this decision."

She hesitated. I held my breath.

"Congratulations, O'Brien," she said. "Welcome to the team!"

The phone slipped from my hand and hit the cushion.

"Hello?" came Coach Riley's muffled voice.

I grabbed the phone. "I'm here!" I shouted. "Sorry, did you just say that I made the team?"

"Good ears," Coach Riley said. "Yes, you made the team, O'Brien."

"But what about my wipeouts?" I asked. "Or the cone drill? I took Dottie's legs out right from under her!"

I bit my lip, instantly regretting my decision to remind her of these unfortunate incidents. To my surprise, Coach Riley laughed.

"Don't you see," she said. "Those are the very reasons why you made the team. Yes, you wiped out. But what did you do after that? You got back up and kept going. That showed me courage. Now, on to the cone drill. Do you really think I didn't know you had some sort of crazy shoulder pad situation going on?"

I cringed.

"I mean, you looked like Quasimodo!" she laughed. "But you did the drill anyway. That showed me determination. Sure, you took a fall. It happens! You also strategized, communicated, and led your team to the finish line. That showed me sportsmanship. Courage, determination, and sportsmanship? Sounds like a winning combo to me."

"But you only played me at center that one time," I said. "All of the other girls tried out a few different positions. I thought that was a bad sign."

"You don't forget a thing, do you, O'Brien?" Coach Riley chuckled. "I played you once because that was all I needed. You are clearly meant to be a center! You're small, fast, and agile, not to mention quick thinking and creative with the puck. Do I need to keep going or will you finally admit that you're good enough to make the team?"

"Yes! Sorry. Count me in!" I said. "Thanks, Coach!"

"Remember," Coach Riley said before hanging up. "Small can still be mighty."

I replayed her words over in my head as I jumped to my feet, eager to share the good news. As I turned around, I saw Dad peeking in the doorway. Billy, Teddy, and Timmy huddled sheepishly on either side of him.

"Sorry," said Dad. "We couldn't resist. Sounds like you got some good news?"

I looked at their smiling faces and couldn't believe I ever doubted them. They would have supported me no matter what. Making the team was an amazing feeling. But knowing I had people who believed in me was an even better one.

The STEAM Expo

"Finally, the moment we've all been waiting for. Welcome to the eighth-grade STEAM Expo!" Doc shouted.

On Friday morning, I stood in the Makerspace nervously waiting for the convention to begin. Doc had rearranged the room with ten tables around the perimeter, each with a competitor and their project. The group was split evenly, five girls and five boys from schools all across the state.

A large group of students, teachers, and parents sat in neatly organized rows in the middle of the room. From their spot in the front, Dad, Billy, Teddy, and Timmy waved nervously.

"You got this!" whispered Louie, flashing me a thumbs-up.

The girls had arrived at the Makerspace early to make sure they got good seats. Rana and Louie made the hockey team too. And Maya's article was scheduled to publish in Sunday's *Cape Chronicle*. We were celebrating tonight with a pajama party.

"It's been an incredible day," Doc continued. "Your teachers and I are so impressed with the work you've done."

We had spent the morning rotating through creative STEAM activities. In the art studio, we learned about 3-D color theory and painted pictures that jumped off of the page when viewed with special glasses. On the playground, we engineered a bridge out of wooden planks to get us from one side of the sandbox to the other. In the computer lab, we programmed robots to perform a funky choreographed dance.

I made new friends and met interesting people who had turned their passion for STEAM into a full-time career. By the time the afternoon rolled around, I had almost completely forgotten about the Expo!

Now, as I looked down at my enhanced set of Extend-O Blades, a hum of energy tingled in my fingertips. The problem I faced when returning to the Makerspace to fix the design had been figuring out what type of safety device would work best.

"I admire your persistence," Doc had said. "That's the sign of a dedicated engineer, Alana. Remember, we take notes for a reason. Why don't you take a look through your notebook? Maybe there's something in there that will be helpful."

Sure enough, I found my answer. It was in my notes from an experiment we did earlier this year.

The challenge had been to use a pile of twigs from the playground to create a stick long enough to flip the light switch on from the other side of the room. In my experiment plan, I had written:

At first, we placed the twigs together end to end and looped tape around them to bind them together. But it wasn't strong enough to support the weight of the twigs as they stretched across the room.

Next, we tried placing strips of tape lengthwise across the two twigs, rather than a loop. But that also didn't work.

Finally, we staggered the twigs on top of one another and looped three sets of tape around the spot where they overlapped. This created a structure strong enough to withstand the gravity and force of being moved up and down.

I decided this was my best option, and got to work building a new set of blades.

This time, I printed twelve C-shaped loops of plastic, each large enough to fit around the blade. Once I fitted the Extend-O Blades to my skates, I glued the loops together with a waterproof glue, giving me six security bars per skate.

Doc tapped the microphone twice, snapping me back to reality. I noticed a ripped patch in the elbow of his lab coat and wondered how it got there.

"Let's get started," he said, "and move full STEAM ahead. Get it? STEAM!"

The audience chuckled as Doc adjusted his glasses.

"The competitors will each have a few minutes now to introduce themselves and give a brief demonstration of their innovative tool," he explained. "Let's start with Alana."

He handed me the wireless microphone. I took a breath and remembered to believe in myself.

"Hello," I began. "My name is Alana O'Brien and my tool is a new twist on an ice hockey blade. Introducing Extend-O Blades! An innovative way to give your smaller-than-average skater added power in the rink."

I spent the next five minutes explaining how I came up with the idea for Extend-O Blades. I also described the steps I took to finish the project.

"As you will see in this short video," I said. "Extend-O Blades are quite strong and can withstand even the bumpiest patch of ice."

I walked to the SMART Board, where my video was waiting, and pressed play.

There, in the center of the screen, was me, skating powerful circles around the Iceberg rink. Billy tossed all sorts of obstacles in my path. I dodged this way and that, expertly maneuvering soccer balls, Hula Hoops, and stuffed animals while the Extend-O Blades remained attached to my blades the whole time. When the screen grew dark, the audience responded with thunderous applause.

"Well done, Miss O'Brien," Doc said, patting me on the back. "Very well done. Now, am I correct in assuming that you came up with this idea during your recent ice hockey tryouts?"

"Yes," I answered. "That's what started it."

"Did you make the team?" asked Doc.

"I did," I answered. "But the funny thing was, I didn't need the Extend-O Blades to do it. Turns out, I had what I needed all along. I think that's what this project really taught me. To believe in myself and always maintain a high level of self-esteem."

I looked at Doc and couldn't resist.

"Get it? STEAM!" I joked.

Doc burst into laughter.

"Good one," he said, snorting. "I'll have to remember that!"

He took the microphone and moved on to the next competitor. The boy held up a tape recorder that translated words into different languages. As he started his presentation, I peeked into the audience. My family and friends smiled at me.

Pretty soon, the competition would be over and the judges would pick a winner. But, somehow, none of that mattered anymore. I was proud of myself and happy with my accomplishments both on and off the ice. Win or lose, despite the bumps in the road, this was one experiment that ended up perfectly according to plan.

ABOUT THE AUTHOR

Brigitte Cooper is a kid lit author, stripes enthusiast and all-around word nerd! She loves sports and once pitched under the bright lights when her Little League softball team, The Dodgers, made the championships! She lives in Greenwich, CT with her kind and funny husband, and enjoys visiting her hometown in Northeastern Pennsylvania. She is lucky to have amazing family, friends, and four furry sidekicks, including an orange kitty named Ginger.

ABOUT THE ILLUSTRATOR

Tim Heitz is an LA based illustrator from St. Louis, Missouri. He began doodling at age 3, went on to receive his Associate in Fine Arts from St. Louis Community College at Florissant Valley and then moved to California, where he finished his studies at San Jose State University, graduating with a Bachelors in Fine Arts (emphasis in animation/illustration). Tim then began his career as a Story Artist in Feature Animation and freelance illustrator for children's books.